Ravished

A Fantasy Omegaverse Romance

Coveted Prey
Book 4

L.V. Lane

Copyright © 2022 L.V. Lane
All rights reserved.
ISBN: 979-8-7363339-7-4

This is a work of fiction. Names, characters, businesses, places, events, and incidents are either the products of the author's imagination or used in a fictitious manner. Any resemblance to actual persons, living or dead, or actual events is purely coincidental.

All rights reserved. This book or parts thereof may not be reproduced in any form, stored in any retrieval system, or transmitted in any form by any means—electronic, mechanical, photocopy, recording, or otherwise—without prior written permission of the author.

Contents

Prologue	1
Chapter 1	5
Chapter 2	21
Chapter 3	37
Chapter 4	49
Chapter 5	57
Also by L.V. Lane	65
About the Author	69

Prologue

Rosalind

"Daughter, may I present to you, Prince Aramis of Torvan."

My father, the King, makes this announcement with a beaming smile, like I should be impressed with my suitor's credentials.

I'm not impressed. This is the fourth noble I've suffered an introduction to within my father's study. A parade forced upon me from the day my scent changed. I welcome the introduction as much as I welcome the ensuing pomp and ceremony.

Which is to say, I don't welcome it at all.

I study Aramis through narrowed, jaundiced eyes. A little brutish, with storm-grey eyes and a military bearing, he cuts an imposing figure. His choice of attire is worthy of note. Leather pants molded to muscular thighs and leather jerkin armor, which, although spotless, lends further evidence to the tales of his barbaric life.

When my perusal of the male offering himself as a

suitor returns to his face, I concede that he is handsome, in a rough, uncivilized sort of way.

My father clears his throat.

"A pleasure, Rosa," Aramis says, performing a formal bow that is not swift enough to hide his smirk.

"Rosa?" I reply, voice ripe with incredulity. Only my closest family dare to call me as such. I hear my father's soft, distressed groan, but I'm incensed by the presumptuousness of Aramis and don't care to temper my response. My eyes narrow—Aramis raises a single brow. He's not a man, I remind myself, he's an alpha, and my recent acquaintance with their kind has set a firm determination that they are all much enamored with their own importance and arrogant to the core.

"My name is Princess Rosalind." My voice has a high, waspish quality that I do not recognize.

"I'll leave you to get acquainted," my father says, already making strides toward his study door.

"Rosa," Aramis repeats as though savoring the word. He dares to wink at me as he takes my hand within his while I'm still wallowing in shock. "I believe it suits your sweet disposition so much better than Rosalind."

Chapter One

Two months later...

Rosalind

Civilized.
 That is the word that comes to mind as I gaze out across the ballroom. Silken gowns in every color of the rainbow, dazzling jewels that sparkle in the lamplight, and dashing gentlemen in smart, dark suits.

A string quartet weaves a melody between the laughter and subtle din of conversation. Beyond the dance floor, the open balcony doors bring the balmy summer breeze and the sweet scent of honeysuckle to wrap around the swaying dancers. On the periphery, men talk, and fans flutter as ladies, old and young, cool faces heated as much from the attention of suitors as the dancing.

Civilized.

On the surface, at least.

I stand in the shadow of my mother, the Queen. Dark

hair with a touch of pure white at her temples, she is the embodiment of regal. She is taller than me by a head and shoulders, as are most people within this room. I'm the third born of five, and my parents' only omega child. My whole life has been one of indulgence... until my scent changed.

Now every beta woman sees me as a threat. Where once the castle women might have offered me a smile, now furtive glances and hushed whispers greet me daily.

Their superstitions make little sense. My scent may be enticing to a beta male, but it will certainly not drive them mad with lust—unlike an alpha.

It matters not that I've no interest in any male, be they alpha or beta. I have become a prisoner of our home, allowed out only under the watch of my parents' most trusted escorts.

"Stephan is a good man," my mother says, head inclining meaningfully toward the tall blond alpha. She is fishing for an answer to the burning question that has been the talk of the castle. "But so is Brent?" She smiles brightly, like it might make the conversation more palatable.

Stephan is a good man, but he's also a weak alpha, and a part of me recoils. Brent is neither a good man nor a good alpha, and I would sooner live with a pig.

Over the last two months it has become painfully apparent that my parents care not which alpha I choose so long as I choose one.

"My dear, you need to pick a suitor," my mother chides softly when I give no answer.

My fan is put to good use cooling my face heated from neither dancing nor the attention of a gallant man.

It is anger that brings a flush to my cheeks; the ever ticking clock never stops taking me forward in unavoidable increments toward my doom.

Ravished

Across the sea lies the Imperium. There, I've been told, a single omega is given over to the care of several alphas—three or four is not uncommon.

I shudder.

Thank the Goddess that I do not live in such a barbarous kingdom. Here it's only one alpha to which I must submit.

One is more than enough.

"Why?" The word is a hiss passing my lips.

Her face softens as though in understanding. Yet she knows nothing of how I feel. My father, her one and only suitor, was her childhood love, and they were betrothed from the age of six. The Goddess smiled with kindness upon my mother's life. She knew nothing of suitors then. Just as she knows nothing of suitors now.

"If you do not pick, my dear, your father will." The same encouraging tone even though I've disobeyed them and taken far longer than is socially acceptable in this matter.

The tone does nothing to soften the blow delivered by those words: my fan stills, the fragile accessory straining under my fierce grip.

Civilized? No, there is nothing civilized about this grand ballroom, nor the many suitors who vie for my hand.

My eyes flash to meet my mother's. They are the same eyes I see when I look in the mirror, just a few more lines gracing the corners. Laughter lines, for my mother smiles and laughs often, at least she used to. Of late, she has not laughed so much, and I know that I'm the cause.

I must choose.

Only words, yet they trap me as effectively as a vise, whiting out the lively tune and conversation and bringing a tightness to my chest. She has never spoken the words before, never admitted my dire fate.

I want the words taken back so that the ignorance might linger longer.

This will be my last all-summer party within my home and castle. The ticking clock tells me I'll not make it to the autumn harvest.

As I meet my mother's steady gaze, I realize that my time is counted in hours rather than days.

"I know." I lower my lashes. "I will give my answer tomorrow."

"My dear child," she says, drawing me into her arms, filling my lungs with the scent of lilies. It comforts me, but it is a false comfort, for tomorrow, I must choose. "The Goddess made you an omega. She has blessed you a thousand times, Rosa. I promise she will not abandon one so cherished. These nerves will pass once you are bound and mated."

Mated, such an ugly, vulgar word that makes me sound no better than a beast. Omegas do not engage in marriage like a beta couple might do. Omegas are a throwback to an era when all humans were shifters, and we lived like animals in caves.

Omegas.

They tell me I'm a coveted prize.

In truth, I'm a nuisance, and they cannot wait for me to leave.

I smile, projecting brightness that I do not feel. "Tomorrow," I say. "Let me have this night."

Her hand presses to my cheek. "Of course. Your father will be so pleased."

She releases me, her joyful smile making me feel wretched to my core.

Ravished

Choose? How can I choose?

I excuse myself under the pretext of some fresh air before I dance again, slipping from the bright lights onto the balcony where guests mingle with waitpersons offering sparkling wine.

I see him instantly—Aramis. His unnaturally pale eyes watch me. They're always watching, waiting. The attractive dark suit cannot disguise what he is.

Ravishment.

That is the word that comes to mind when I think about Aramis.

Deep in the night, as I lay alone upon my bed, my thoughts turn toward what it might be like to be with such a man.

Where I am smaller, he is larger: an alpha to an omega in a room awash with betas. A female omega is not like an ordinary beta woman, for we crave rough treatment—we have needs that only an alpha can sate.

Or so I have been told.

He is one of many alphas here. They come to vie for me with sweet words and the facade of humility.

They are neither sweet nor humble. They are monsters and beasts who watch with predatory intent.

He is the worst of them—Aramis. *He* is the one I'll never choose.

And why would I? It's well known he only petitions for my hand to facilitate his claim to a wealthy duchy. A childless uncle has died, and his widow, now past child-bearing age, must select an heir from their two nephews.

Aramis is the only claimant to be an alpha. But his cousin has wedded a beta and they already have three heirs.

The criteria with which the widow must decide upon an heir remains a mystery—so far she chooses neither.

And now Aramis pursues me in a quest to tip the scales in his favor.

I snort out my disdain, snatching a glass from a proffered tray. The bubbles tickle my throat, and I gulp more than savor the sweet, sparkling wine.

We are separated by a great distance, he on one side of the balcony in conversation with his companion, Edgar, and I on the other, alone. Yet, he knows my intent to choose another. I can see it in the tightening of his jaw and the narrowing of his eyes.

Who would ever pick such a dominant male, even were his intentions true? Not me. Thin lips that the ladies call rakish when he smiles, dark hair, and storm-grey eyes. His shoulders are broad and powerful, muscular thighs, broad, booted feet, and Goddess save me from the image of his tight ass filling his pants whenever I glimpse him from behind.

But there is more to Aramis than his striking appearance, for he has the heart of an alpha and has fought in many distant wars.

And therein lies the crux of the matter—he is too much alpha even ignoring his lack of virtue, and I would surely wilt under the influence of such a man.

I shiver under his inspection. I should move or turn away, yet I am caught, as I've been many times, by that unwavering gaze.

He is the antonym of civilized.

He is barely contained brutality.

He is basal and cruel in ways I cannot dare to comprehend, yet instinct tells me is true.

Tomorrow, I must choose.

Tonight is mine.

Ravished

Aramis

She is plotting something, my little doe.

The tightening of the leash has brought the feral in her rising to the surface. I hide my smile, taking a sip from the tall, fluted glass.

"She's plotting," Edgar says, nudging his head at Princess Rosalind.

"I know," I say. "The question is, what?"

"I've heard she'll choose Stephan tomorrow," he says.

I choke on my drink. He smirks, the bastard might be a beta, but he has never been afraid to offer a jibe. "She will not pick Stephan. She'll not pick anyone, and tomorrow her father will fulfill his promise to me."

He raises a brow. "Have you not heard? Her father has issued her an ultimatum."

"He has?" This news does not please me. I've given over a great deal of time and effort to ensure the King selects me as her mate. "I did not think the King had the balls to force her hand?"

"She must choose, or he will." He gestures toward Rosa. "Does that look like a woman about to yield to you?"

No, it does not.

"She will not choose you," Edgar continues. "She'll pick Stephan—he is the weakest."

"I will challenge him if she does."

He sighs, drawing my brooding attention. "It will not end well if you do. And then your plans to rule your uncle's duchy will be over."

I raise my brows. "Are you telling me I should forfeit? Bow out?"

As the only alpha in a beta family, I've lived a troubled life. I am not firstborn and deference is not in my nature. Restless by circumstance, I'm never satisfied with any place or situation. I've traveled far, sailed seas, and fought in many wars. Edgar, my childhood friend, has been at my side through it all.

I do not fit in the civilized world.

I'm a throwback to an era when we were more beast than human.

At times I feel more like a beast when my darkness overtakes my humanity, and I succumb to urges for violence or debauchery.

My parents and extended family, all gentle betas, are ever disappointed in me.

So it came as a surprise to everyone when my uncle named me in his will. The duchy is small in terms of land but includes several profitable mineral mines.

That profit comes at a cost, for late every autumn, Orc raiding parties come to harry the supply lines.

It needs a strong leader. I'd thought myself beyond such things, a wanderer doomed to die somewhere far away fighting a war for people I cared naught about. An alpha was never meant to be a second son, but I find a new purpose in the chance to rule and protect a duchy.

I want this opportunity more than I've wanted anything in my life.

Unfortunately, my uncle's will included two potential successors to the estate. Gerald, a distant cousin, is also named, and my widowed aunt was instructed to choose between us before summer's end.

Gerald, a beta, offers stability in that he has a wife and three children.

But I'm the alpha.

Ravished

My basal side rails that he should even be considered over me, and I pity the duchy residents should Gerald prevail given he has a reputation for bumbling every project his father has set him.

I cannot and will not let the lands go to him.

What better way to tip the scales toward my rightful success than to take an omega and a princess as my mate?

So, here I came, seeking to secure a princess so that I might secure a duchy lest it be claimed by my sniveling cousin.

But everything changed after I met her.

My lips tug up as I recall the dressing down she gave me when I dared to call her Rosa the day we first met. Her eyes spitting fire at me like a heathen had entered her father's study and not an alpha and prince.

Her scent has captivated me, her beauty more so. And those haughty looks she throws my way whenever I engage her in conversation bring my dominant nature rearing to the surface. I don't want a sweet beta—I can think of nothing worse. Rather, I want to tame my little doe with the heart of a lioness. I want to put her over my lap and spank her until her bottom turns a fiery shade of red and she begs for mercy. And I want to watch that petulant mouth open on a breathy gasp as I fill her sweet pussy with my cock.

We are separated by a distance, yet I see rebellion in every tense line of her body.

I'm utterly beguiled by the willful omega. And I will be the one who brings her to heel.

"I can no more bow out than I can cut off my own dick," I say.

Edgar snorts a laugh. "What friend would I be counseling you in such a path, even supposing I believed you might abandon your desires? Your Aunt Grace is here, is she not?"

I nod. I admit to believing it a good sign when my aunt arrived last week and hoped it meant she looked favorably upon my actions.

"This is no coincidence," Edgar continues. "I'm certain the wily widow is only holding back on a decision to force your hand in seeking a match—your sweet omega is not the only female to engage in plotting. Grace is a close friend to the Queen; they have been meeting daily since her arrival. No, you must, if need be, eliminate the competition in a more civilized way before Rosa chooses tomorrow."

"Civilized? Have we not been friends for many years? I've not been civilized a single day of my life."

He smirks and claps a hand upon my shoulder. "It does not need to *be* civilized, only to *seem* civilized. You have faked it this far, have you not?"

I laugh. "Clearly, I've not faked it well enough... I believe I'm owed a dance with my sweet little doe," I say, giving my empty glass to a passing waitperson. "After, I shall follow your wise counsel and dissuade her other suitors by whatever means is necessary."

꙳

Rosalind

Aramis is walking straight toward me.

No, he is *stalking* straight toward me with a determined expression on his face that induces an instant and unwelcoming clouding of my thoughts.

I'm supposed to dance with my suitors. It's my duty to

dance with them, but damn my duty to hell, for I do not want to dance with *him*.

I turn in a full circle finding predatory gazes in every direction.

"Going somewhere, Princess?"

I freeze as his presence dominates the space directly behind me. "Yes," I say. The mental malady afflicting me provides me with no destination.

Glancing over my shoulder, I cut him a glare. My waspish disposition is like fuel upon his flames, and he only smirks before rounding to stand before me where he claims my hand.

"I was about to—dance," I say, then curse my bluff when his smile turns wolfish.

"An excellent idea," he says, standing close enough now for his rich, spicy alpha pheromones to saturate my nose and lungs. "I have yet to claim my dance."

All night, I have felt the weight of my other watchers, but for the first time, I feel safe within Aramis's shadow as he guides me to the dancefloor.

There is nothing inappropriate about the hand he places at my waist as we join the other swaying dancers. Yet, I'm breathless in ways that go beyond the exertion of a gentle dance. The Goddess issued a cruel twist when she made an omega susceptible to an alpha's scent, and I refuse to linger on the possibility that it might be something more.

Nature's manipulation of my will brings out my rebellious side. Stiffness enters my posture, and an involuntary growl escapes my lips.

Aramis chuckles, his head lowering until his lips graze my ear. "Sweet Rosa, if you understood how much an alpha enjoys spirit in his mate, you would not throw so many gauntlets at my feet."

I swallow against the sudden dryness in my throat. Somehow, I make it through the dance without tripping over my feet or slapping his arrogant face.

Then he is excusing himself and striding off, and Stephan arrives to take his place. Where Aramis's scent brings a tingle, Stephan's is thick and cloying.

Why do I only notice this now?

As the dance ends, it's Brent who takes Stephan's place. Brent who holds me too tight, and who takes the opportunity to remind me of the importance of an omega's submission.

Brent is aggressive. I sense Aramis has equal capacity for this trait, yet he has shown me, an omega, only measured dominance.

Brent does not enjoy my spirit, nor the challenge it represents unless it's a precursor to him breaking my will. As he paws at me in a way that I'm sure will leave bruises, I reflect that there is a difference between dominance and aggression—not all alphas are equal.

I excuse myself after this dance, only to blunder into my older sister by five years, Elisa.

One day she will be queen and her husband king through marriage. She cannot wait to be rid of me, for she sees my omega status as a threat.

All because her husband is an alpha.

I'm no threat to her. It's *he* who is a threat to me.

"Was it you who spoke to Father?" I demand. She is taller than our mother, willow thin, and considered the most beautiful woman in the kingdom. One day she will be queen; one would think these blessings enough.

"Elijah would not even look at you were it not for your scent," she says. "You are a temptation the Goddess herself placed upon this earth. You need to be mated. Only then will your scent change and this episode of madness end." She shrugs one delicate shoulder. "I told our father that he must select an alpha for you, or you must be sent away."

"Father would not send me away," I say, but as I see her cold smile, I know it for a possibility.

Heat fills my cheeks that she would dare to make such a proposal.

"You are third born," she says coldly. "And nothing were you not an omega."

She pivots on the spot and sashays back toward her waiting attendants who cluster around her the moment she arrives.

Once upon a time, I had willing attendants whom I could call my friends. Now I'm nothing but an annoyance.

My nails press into my palms until the sting grows sharp enough to rouse me. I wallow between compassion and hatred for the way Elisa has treated me since I came of age. I tell myself there are two sides to everything. That she is only bitter that her husband is obsessed with me and will not take his wife to bed anymore. That his lack of attention is a double blow, for she is desperate to get with child to better secure her position as queen when the time comes.

But none of this is my fault.

And I'm not yet ready to choose.

The evening passes in torturous minutes—I count every one.

I perform my royal duty. I dance with more suitors, chat with the few ladies I can still call friends, and smile my brightest smile whenever I catch my parents' eyes.

But the night is drawing to a close, and tomorrow I must choose. Inside, nerves flutter as I slip into the edges of the ballroom seeking a few moments of blessed peace.

"Are you enjoying your party, Rosalind?"

I step back, eyes lifting warily as Elijah looms before me.

"You should not be here," I say, pulse fluttering and eyes darting from side to side, searching for an escape.

"Here?" He plants his palms against the wall to either side of me, trapping me. "This is my home. Soon I will be king. It could be your home too, were you to choose to stay. Your sister would have no choice but to accept you, were you carrying my child."

A disdainful snort escapes me despite a firm belief that antagonizing the alpha will not end well. Then he dares to put his hand upon my arm, and I slap his face with all my small strength. "Do not touch me!" I hiss.

His face twists: shock, anger, and the promise of retaliation.

"Elijah?" My sister's call offers a distraction, and I use the moment to flee. As I run, the clock strikes midnight and the fireworks bloom to celebrate all-summer night.

I should be happy, but I'm desolate in the wake of what might have come to pass if not for my sister's timely arrival.

Hot tears spill down my cheeks as I run on, leaving the festivities for the shadows of the forest.

Chapter Two

Aramis

My evening has proven busy as I track down Rosa's many suitors one by one, ensuring they all understood it's time for them to withdraw—by whatever means is necessary. Elijah, the alpha who would one day be king, has also met with my bloody wrath.

As the all-summer party draws to a close in the early hours of the morning, I stand over the prone body of my last opponent, breathing heavy and blood heated with the joy of violent victory.

This is how it is meant to be.

Omegas are few, and they should go only to those most worthy.

No alpha likes to concede defeat. This last, and most challenging fight, was both long and bloody. A few witnesses linger to help my opponent—other alphas and the occasional beta who offer adjudication and validity to my victory.

Tomorrow, my little doe will have no one to choose but me.

I smile, imagining her shocked gasp as I present myself as the only mate, face and knuckles proudly bruised in evidence of how I've challenged others for the position.

She will have no choice.

And really, can I call myself an alpha and allow a princess and omega to be claimed in any other way?

The pain brings a heightened sense of awareness. False pretenses of societal progress dictate we hide our alpha side. But how good it feels to unleash it from the cloying restraints, if only for a short time.

Edgar's arrival does not stir me so much as the pallor of his face. The fury barely easing after my fight rises in answer to this silent call.

"She has fled," he says, voice a whisper, eyes shifting from me to the small gathering. "We cannot delay. She has left for the portal."

I cannot believe she would be so foolish as to enter, yet I also do not believe wholly that she will not.

We ride hard along the forest path that she has traveled on foot a short time ago.

Rage consumes me. At her mother and father for not guarding their treasure well before she is entrusted to her alpha. At the petulant, spoiled brat who would do something so reckless. At myself, for letting down my guard and allowing distraction to creep in the form of the night's many challenges.

The distance is short. Our horses take the narrow forest path at a canter, but as it opens out and both portal and my little doe come into view, we shift to a gallop.

Billowing summer-blue skirts that match her eyes are caught in the grasp of her hands making waves behind her, hair escaping the pretty arrangement in long tendrils. Face turning, her eyes widen as she sees our approach and she doubles down on her flight.

She is too close to the portal.

I'm too far away.

"You must pass through at the same time!" Edgar calls, his slower horse losing ground to mine.

"You think I don't know that!" My voice is a growl as I urge my gelding to his limit and beyond.

Rage gives way to a fear so cold it grips me like the harshest winter wind.

I cannot lose her now—not like this.

My pounding approach only spurs her on to greater speed. Desperation chokes me—she cannot possibly know what lies on the other side. No one can; it is the nature of the portal.

A wild sea, a barren desert, a horde of demons. Nothing is impossible once you cross that shimmering gate.

Her reaching hand is swallowed first, followed by her head, shoulders, and body.

As the last wisp of her billowing skirts traverse that ancient boundary, my brave horse's muzzle makes contact, and we plunge together into the abyss.

 ❦

Rosalind

I have seen the portal often, living as we do so close to the ancient site. I've heard about the portal, too, from brave travelers who return with tales from the other side.

It's as wondrous as it is terrifying.

Many leave for adventure.

Sometimes they return.

More often, they're never seen again.

I flee for the portal site in a state of great uncertainty. In truth, I want only to look upon the possibility of a simpler life that might await me on the other side.

I've heard monsters roam desolate lands.

I've heard stories of utopia.

And everything in between.

You never really know.

But it's also said that you can feel the presence of the Goddess close to the portal. Many pilgrims travel from the far corners of the world to pay homage to the Mother of All Things. I've never sought her counsel before, but tonight, as I face the greatest decision of my short life, I need *Her* guidance.

My plan to gaze upon possibilities, to kneel before the ancient site and seek comfort from the Goddess, is thwarted by the arrival of Aramis and his companion.

The sight of the two riders charging toward me shoots ice into my spine. An age-old instinct drives me to run from the alpha. The how or why he's here and pursues me is lost under this imperative toward flight.

A form of madness grips me—a desire to test the man who I recognize in this wild moment to be my one true alpha.

Perhaps it's the influence of the Goddess so close to the portal that brings belated clarity to my turbulent thoughts.

Stephan, I understand now, was never fated to be with me.

Aramis is the strongest suitor.

The most dominant.

The most worthy.

Ravished

I can admit this now as I flee for the portal that I never intend to pass through.

He will catch me before I tumble into the abyss. How could the Goddess allow anything else?

Yet, as the shimmering gate nears amid the thunder of approaching hooves and Aramis's roars for me to stop, I realize that the Goddess has other plans.

I am too close to the portal.

He will not catch me in time.

Caution dictates I stop.

I do not. Reckless faith in the Mother of All Things urges my feet to faster flight.

And as the shimmering wall envelopes me in its cool, oily embrace, I finally wonder at my mistake.

§

The tumbling seems to last an eternity. Falling, falling, twisting, and crashing until my battered body screams in protest.

Finally, it stops.

Stopping is a shock.

A horse screams. A low, masculine rumble offers comfort, and as I lift myself from the ground to my hands and knees, I see Aramis fighting to calm his rearing horse.

My stomach heaves, bringing up watery wine and bile. I'm utterly wretched in this moment.

When I'm finally done with my misery, a waterskin lands on the ground before me. My hand shakes as I wipe my mouth before snatching up the bag. Rinsing my mouth, I spit the foul taste out and, sinking back onto my heels, take a long gulp.

My eyes remain lowered, cheeks heated with shame.

I'm still in the same forest, the same dirt path beneath me. I cannot readily decide if Aramis stopped me or the Goddess herself sealed the portal door.

My parents will be furious.

Everyone will be furious.

A pair of broad, booted feet enter my view. I do not want to look up, but steeling myself, I do.

Thin lips make a cruel line as he stares down at me. He appears impossibly huge as I regard him from this vulnerable position upon the ground. I'm as shocked to see the evidence of violence upon his face as I am by the empty expression. I try not to wonder how he came to appear so, but I do, and my suspicions chill me to the core.

"I thought I'd passed through," I say. My voice sounds small, and I suffer great sorrow and guilt at what I tried to do.

"Through?" His face is so very stern now that I hardly recognize the alpha who always played at civilized with me.

I start to speak, then stop. My shaking fingers knead at my temple. A prickling sense of malaise creeps under my skin as I look around—something is wrong. Yet, it's all as I expect: the dark of night, the hoot of a distant owl, the warm summer air, and the forest bracing the path.

A high keening wail rises from the darkness to my left. We both turn to face it.

I shudder, my brows drawing together in a frown. It's the sound of grief and of death.

Cursing softly under his breath, Aramis strides to his horse and draws forth a sword stowed against the saddle.

"What?" My mouth is so dust-dry that I can barely get the word out. "What was that?"

When he turns back to me, he shrugs, heavy shoulders lifting. The sword is gripped loosely in his right hand, but his body is alert. "I do not know, Princess." His free hand turns over, fingers making an upward motion.

I rise gracelessly to my feet.

Wrong.

The sense of malaise is like a slow, creeping tide washing over my body. I turn full circle. "Where has it gone?" The source of my anxiety manifests in the absence of the portal.

His grunt is derisive.

Another long, desolate wail rises from the shadowy forest.

"Portals do not wait for us to hop back and forth," he says. "Were it so easy, we would do it all the time. The one you used has moved. And even should you find it, it would likely not take you home, but rather somewhere more terrible than this."

This does not seem so terrible. It's a forest and a mirror of the one we've just left. I'm still in a state of confusion, and perhaps denial, that I've truly left my kingdom.

A distant roar, as alien as the deathly wail, confirms this is not my home anymore.

"Do you know nothing of the portal laws, Princess?" he says, placing his larger bulk between me and the threat.

I shake my head. I've had very little interest in the portal other than listening to the fanciful tales of those who have traveled to worlds on the other side. On occasion, I did wonder if they were merely skilled bards who hadn't ventured through the portal at all.

"You know as little of your laws as you do of alphas and omegas." There is censure in his voice. "You're a spoiled, selfish brat who has never once been held accountable for your behavior." He glances back, stormy grey eyes holding mine, and I dare not look away. "That is about to change."

I'm about to remind him that I've yet to choose, and when I *do* choose, it will assuredly not be him, when a snarling mass explodes from the trees: thick, black fur, white teeth, the body of a wolf but as large as a horse.

I fear my eyes deceive me, but no, it really has three heads.

The horse rears and bolts for the undergrowth.

Aramis raises his sword and charges to meet the creature. His blade swings. The monster lunges, snapping jaws, clawed paws gouging the rough ground.

Thrust and slash. Snarl and snap.

They weave back and forth, side to side, neither gaining advantage nor ground, and all the while I'm rooted to the spot.

Aramis's blade glances the beast's hind leg, and it howls, savage heads rearing and jaws snapping. Sometimes the three wolf heads work in unison, and sometimes they take turns.

His blade swings again. The monster retreats and then leaps.

Another howl pierces the night as he slashes the throat of the rightmost head. It falls limp. The two remaining wolf heads rise for a howl that promises bloody revenge.

They circle and fight.

A desperate dance of life and death.

I want to help. I want to run and hide, but shock has me in its grip, and I do neither of those things.

The beast snarls its anger.

Aramis growls back.

Goddess save us. We are going to die.

My eyes lower, searching the ground for a weapon... for a distraction, for anything that might help. A small branch is all I see, and I snatch it up wondering how I might put it to use.

"Get back," Aramis growls as if sensing my intent. He charges once more, the sword dipping under the rearing beast and impaling deep into its chest.

A high keening wail accompanies it crashing to the ground. Blood sprays from the mortal wound. The beast flails, the dread heads thrashing as Aramis hacks and chops, throwing up great fountains of blood.

With a final piteous wail, the wolf-beast heaves its last breath and stills.

I watch Aramis's back heave with deep, fierce breaths.

Then he turns, eyes narrowing on the crude weapon in my hands.

I drop it.

Goddess help me, he has slain this impossible creature.

His fine clothes are shredded. Tossing the sword to the ground, he strips the tunic over his head and drops it beside his sword.

Rivulets of blood escape a gash left by claws. His chest continues to heave, sweat glistening over the tan skin as his eyes lock with mine.

The urge to prostrate myself at his feet is strong. He is godlike in this moment, all-powerful.

He is both a monster and my savior.

His scent saturates the air, and I lick my lips, tasting it.

It is utterly delicious. I sway a little like I have eaten too many moon berries.

A smile lights his lips as steady steps bring him toward me. "Stop fighting your nature," he says. "And this will go so much easier, Princess."

I blink, trying to lift myself from the strange daze that is settling upon me. As he nears, more of his rich, spicy scent fills my lungs. It radiates outward, instilling a low, nervous swarm of butterflies deep in the pit of my belly.

Goddess, his scent is heavenly. My legs grow weak, and standing is nigh impossible.

My hand lowers to my stomach, where the fluttering assaults me.

What is happening?

He growls. Not the vicious kind that he used in a challenge to the monster. This is low, more of a purr, and it sends the butterflies into a frenzy.

"It's time for your punishment," he says ominously.

I swallow. I'm sure the devil has possessed him to make such an announcement mere moments after he has slain a beast. Have I not been punished enough by the circumstance of being trapped in a parallel world?

The butterflies abandon me, and my stomach performs a slow clench.

"Punishment?" I ask. My pulse leaps and my palms turn a little clammy.

His smile widens as he cups my cheek. The shock of his touch and the proprietary nature sets off little explosions under my skin. Where Elijah's touch filled me with revulsion, Aramis's is comfort. "Will you accept your discipline like a good girl?"

I shake my head. His warm palm is smothering my will. "I didn't mean to pass through the portal," I say, strengthening my resolve against the magic of his touch. I step backward, breaking the connection. "I'm a princess. It's not your place to punish me, even supposing it were necessary—which it's not."

He stalks after me. I step back, stumbling over a root.

"This is madness."

"Is it, Princess?"

Ravished

I'm backing up with haste now, but he's a predator honing in upon his prey. I lose my footing.

He catches my arm within his fist before I fall.

Then I do fall, for the world tilts as he takes a seat upon a nearby fallen tree and tosses me face first over his lap.

"Goddess! Unhand me at once!"

A firm swat lands against my silk-covered ass and startles a yelp from me.

"Had you not been so foolish, I would be claiming you tomorrow. It is absolutely my right to punish you in any way I see fit. And believe me, Princess *Rosa*. You will be repentant long before I'm satisfied."

I know all the reasons for his beaten face in that instant. I'd fooled myself into thinking I had some choice in this, that he would not fall to his natural, basal side that I've always suspected was there.

I'm terrified, yet I cannot deny excitement lights a fire inside my core. My conflict manifests in a fierce struggle and desire to resist.

It is over with embarrassing swiftness, and my silk skirts are thrust up, smothering my head as sharp, stinging smacks are peppered over my upturned bottom.

Once the first few heat my skin, he takes his time with the punishment, seeming to savor each carefully placed spank. My pussy begins to clench with each clap of his massive hand. He takes longer between, pausing to pet and pinch the smarting flesh.

At first, it's my shame that makes me struggle and cry out. Soon the fiery pain spreads and builds, and my shocked gasps turn to tears that are as much frustration as genuine hurt.

As I wriggle, I can feel slick gathering where my thighs squeeze together.

His fingers linger for longer between the spanks. I find myself holding my breath as they pass close to the swollen folds protected from his touch by the flimsy barrier of my panties.

They are wet, too.

I can feel them sticking to my pussy, and to the tops of my thighs.

"Open your legs," he commands.

I do not open my legs.

But a rain of sharp, stinging blows to my sensitive sit-spot soon changes my mind.

The next three spanks land upon my silk covered pussy. I clench with each and every one, the pain near orgasmic. Goddess help me, do I imagine that it sounds wet?

It's not enough that I'm humiliated and mastered already, for he pauses to explore the damp silk. A low purr emanates from his chest as he presses the silk into me and then gently tugs it away. His purr deepens as he repeats this. "Can you feel that, Princess? Your pretty silk panties are all stuck up inside you." He presses a thick finger against my throbbing entrance, forcing the material in before tugging it back out again. "These will need to come off before I can finish your punishment."

Barely do I mumble my protest when my panties are tugged all the way down, over my booted feet, and tossed to the ground before he resumes spanking my naked flesh.

I sob, and I plead. He is unmoved and determined to chastise me in the sternest, most severe manner a man can.

This time when the smacks veer toward my pussy, the wet clapping sound is unmistakable.

"What a naughty little Princess," he says.

I groan and strain for more as his thick fingers glide over the burning, sensitized flesh of my outer pussy lips where I weep for his attention. I'm throbbing everywhere, my head and face hot and flushed from my storm of tears, my body exhausted from my flight.

I desperately want to come.

Disappointment fills me as he withdraws, and lowering my skirts, he helps me to unsteady feet.

I hear a distant, soft whinny coming from the forest. At Aramis's whistle, his horse comes trotting through to join us on the path. The horse tosses its head and whinnies again as it sees the slain beast, shying before trotting toward his master's outstretched hand. Gathering the reins, Aramis soothes the frightened animal with soft words and a gentle stroke along the horse's neck. I'm relieved to see the horse well. But I'm also reminded that this place is not safe.

"Come," Aramis says. Collecting his sword and ruined shirt, he tucks them against the horse's saddle before turning to me. "We cannot linger on this path."

With my hand in his, we walk a little distance into the dark forest, my eyes and ears straining for sounds of a threat. The feel of his larger, callused hand around mine is comforting, but it also unsettles me. I thought I understood this man, but events have ripped that small amount of certainty away.

The sound of rushing water greets us before we come out to the side of a small pool. Night makes it both eerie and magical. The horse snorts once before lowering his head to drink.

Aramis removes the saddle and bridle, leaving me momentarily alone.

What will we do now? This place cannot possibly be safe.

Yet, it's not concerns for my safety that fill my mind, but the awareness of the alpha who tends to his horse with low soothing words and gentle coaxing hands. Mesmerized, I watch the play of muscles across his sculptured back, the broad, capable hands that have left a lingering ache on my bottom and have touched me intimately.

The butterflies are back. The softly beating wings soon become a ripple that twists up into a savage cramp.

Goddess help me. I'm rendered momentarily deaf and blind as I'm caught within the fist of the pain.

Aramis has saved me, only to watch me die.

Chapter Three

Aramis

I see the moment her heat takes her. A soft gasp and her sudden pallor before her face contorts.

My growl is one of encouragement as she doubles over before sinking to her knees.

The vicious cramping in her stomach is the first of many steps. Pain is necessary. It's part of life. It's integral to the dance between an alpha and an omega.

It's her body preparing for me, her mate.

I rejoice in her suffering, for it will open her for the pleasure to come.

"Goddess help me, what is happening?" Her anxious, hissed whisper draws me to offer comfort. My rough hand strokes over her silken hair, my growl shifting to a purr as she presses into my open palm, seeking more. "Please, I don't understand. I feel so empty."

My cock thickens and lengthens. Rosa's small hands clutch her stomach, although it will not ease the ache. "Little fool," I say not unkindly. "You have fled the safety of your home on the cusp of your awakening. This will be rough on you, Princess. There is nothing that can be done about that. Had you only submitted to me willingly, I would have taken you with the care your innocent body deserves." Pretty tears fall down her cheeks, her body trembling as the awakening takes her deeper into its embrace. "No opportunity for soft-things that an omega in heat craves—no nest. Now, it will be an entirely different kind of heat you must endure for I can offer you no comforts here."

"Please," she says as tremors wrack her body.

I pet her hair as nature takes its course, smoothing out the tangles and the few pins that have survived her tumble through the portal. When I lift her chin that I might better see the emotions playing upon her face, her cornflower-blue eyes plead with me to take this terrible suffering away.

And I will.

"Oh!" Her hands sink lower. "Goddess!"

The scent of slick drives a stoniness to my cock already painfully aroused and trapped behind my leather pants. I breathe deeply, drawing her pheromones into my lungs, and welcoming the haze of my burgeoning rut.

Her face turns, nose sinking into the leather at my crotch—small hands fumble at my belt.

My purr shifts to a growl as she frees my aching shaft.

She gasps as she frees me, eyes widening and lips parting on a little 'O'. Her small hands are unable to fully close around my girth. I'm sure she's about to balk or scream or both, but she leans forward, closes her eyes, and licks the leaking tip.

My eyes roll back—it's all I can do to resist snatching her up. The sensation of her wet tongue gently lapping all around the sensitive tip brings instant tightness to my balls.

The pleasure is maddening—I want desperately to fist her pretty hair and plug her throat until she chokes.

I don't. Instead, I steel myself for this tentative torment, watching her sweet face turn to rapture as she laps my leaking seed.

"Good girl," I encourage, stroking her hair as she tastes me.

Greedy now, she sucks me deeper, pretty cheeks hollowing and flushing as my essence is drawn into her belly. My cock spits near constantly, giving her body what is needed to see her fully embrace her heat.

She sucks me deeper still, choking herself in her enthusiasm for my cock and cum.

I'm an alpha about to claim my one and only mate, and a deep-rooted imperative demands I do so thoroughly, despite the circumstance.

The vision of her small mouth stretched around my fat cock head is intensely captivating, her enthusiasm equally so.

While I allow her to dictate our coupling so far, she must learn all sides of me.

That I can be a gentle and patient lover.

But that I'm an alpha first and foremost, and that I will always know what she needs.

Her hooded eyes widen as I take her glorious hair as a leash. She hums around my cock, and my lips tug up in a smirk of pure masculine joy. Were she a beta sensing my nefarious intentions, she would be quaking in terror. But Rosa is an omega, sent by the Goddess herself to slake an alpha's lust. Now, she is mine and only mine, and she'll embrace every debauch game I play and beg me for more.

"Do you understand that when an alpha claims his mate, he must take her in every way?" I force my cock deeper as I speak, growling with pleasure as her throat closes around it. "That he will mark his mate all over her pretty body?" I begin to fuck her pretty mouth harder, driving my length into her tight throat with each thrust.

Her small hands cling to my hips, and her eyes boldly meet mine. Her heat has taken her swiftly, animal instincts taking over human intellect. "Swallow around me, love, and you will be able to take more." Goddess save me, she does, and I grit my teeth to hold back the boiling storm rising in my balls. Her wet tongue laves me with every passage of my cock, small hands clenching, trying to take me deeper still.

Spit and pre-cum soon leak over her chin, tears stream from her eyes, but she is a greedy omega, already subject to the haze of heat, and she needs to be taken roughly.

She hums. Nails raking my hip. I feel the tingle in the base of my spine. The heady rush as my cum ejaculates down her tight throat weakens my legs and sets my whole body shaking. She chokes, gasps, swallows, and chokes again. I try to ease from her tightness, but her small hands clutch as she sucks upon her treat, forcing me to pinch her cheeks before she frees me.

She growls at being denied. I give her a shake, utterly beguiled as I hold the little feral kitten from her prize lest she hurt herself. But my cock is still spilling cum, and I retain possession of rationality by the slimmest of threads.

Then sanity leaves me, for she licks her lips and swipes fingers over her sticky chin before stuffing them into her mouth.

Rosalind

My body is on fire, and my intellect is focused on the powerful male who stands over me. His scent fills my nose and lungs, and his taste makes my mouth water. I've dreamt of his face, his hands, and of his muscular body moving over mine, although I've tried hard to forget it.

It's inevitable that we should be here.

"I want more," I demand as I stare up at him from where I kneel at his feet.

I spare only the briefest glance toward his face for my interest is all on the thick ruddy cock jutting proudly from a nest of dark curls. My pussy clenches as I note the faint swelling near the base where the skin is a darker crimson color.

His knot.

Deep inside, I throb with need, slick with my arousal so that it might ease his possession. My lips are sore, and my throat aches, but were he not fisting my hair, I would fall greedily upon him all over again.

I growl my displeasure. Aramis roars back, a menacing sound that makes my body tremble and my pussy weep.

His lips tug up at the corners in a smile that promises wickedness of the highest order. "Don't worry, Princess. I will see you well rutted through your heat." He shakes me again, but it only makes me groan.

Fist in my hair, he takes me down onto the loamy forest floor. My dress is thrust up, and his thick fingers penetrate my core.

"Goddess, yes!"

My legs fall apart, hips lifting as I strain to get more.

"I'm not sure you're ready," he says with maddening calm. His other hand grips the neckline of my dress and tugs it down until my small breasts bounce free. With a dark smile upon his lips, he leans down and takes the tight nipple and half my breast into the warm cavern of his mouth.

And sucks.

My back rises off the ground, my pussy clenches over the thrusting fingers that slam in and out wetly.

I'm lost. The pleasure is like a golden thread pulling with each rhythmic suck and wet thrust until I shatter into blissful contractions and a scream. He doesn't stop, keeps thrusting and twisting his thick fingers into my greedy pussy, while white-hot pleasure shoots from my breast to my groin. My hips undulate as I thrash upon the floor. My pussy gushes over his hand, but I still want more.

His lips pop off, and he moves attention to the other breast, marking sharp love-bites over the plump mound before taking the needy nipple into his mouth and sucking hard. My fingers bury in his hair; my nails rake his scalp.

It's then that the terrible cramping claims me once again.

I'm on fire.

I'm burning from the inside out.

His head lifts, silver-grey eyes holding mine. I want to curl into a ball and hide, but he takes my wrists, pinning them within a single hand, high above my head.

"Good girl," he says, fingers scissoring inside me, stretching me. "Give yourself over to your heat."

The cramping is all-consuming. I'm sure I'm about to die, here on this filthy forest floor.

As swiftly as the cramps arrive, they leave, and I pant in the aftermath. "Please," I beg. "I need more."

His smile is pure calculation as whatever control holds him, snaps. Strong hands grasp the neck of my pale blue ballgown. He rips. Material tears in a violent rush, and tiny pearl buttons pop and scatter across the forest floor. He takes a fresh handful and tugs, again and again, stripping dress, petticoats, stockings, and boots from me.

Several long strips are torn from one of the petticoats, and a rough bed of sorts is made with the remainder of my ruined dress and underthings—I'm tossed to the middle, wrists soon bound and impaled to the ground with his dagger.

I fight with all my small strength, but each ankle is similarly bound, spreading me wide, knees bent open like a lewd sacrifice upon the ground. The ache inside me is growing, a terrible emptiness that must find relief.

The last of his clothes are stripped away as I lay panting upon the ground, half-delirious, desperate, and needy for the thick cock hanging between his legs. My stomach ripples in echoes of pleasure, my pussy feels open and slick. I test the bonds as I watch the resplendent alpha prowl before me, delighted when I find escape impossible. He rolls his shoulders as he stalks back toward me, thick muscles bunching and rippling.

His eyes never leave mine, chest heaving, eyes pitch-black, and expression empty.

"Now," he says as he comes down over me. "I will rut you through your heat."

The sensation of him crowding over me is welcoming. I'm vulnerable before this huge male, yet his powerful body provides a cage inside which I'm safe. Hot flesh, far thicker than his fingers, slides through the copious slickness between my legs before the tip slowly sinks inside.

I breathe in his rich pheromones, twitching under him, restless, feeling the ripple of straining muscles that part for his cock. Lips take a heated trail up my throat, bringing sobs of joy. My thoughts splinter between the lips at my throat and his burning flesh sinking ever deeper into me. The more he surrounds me, the deeper I fall into a carnal fog.

My breath stutters. I fret, straining against the bindings, then hiss as his cock head nudges against the barrier of my virginity. A broad hand finds my hip and tilts my pelvis. My knees are bent and open; I have nowhere to go.

I can only submit.

"No other man or alpha will touch you once you bear my mark," he growls against my throat. Then his hips roll back and slam forward, filling me entirely in a single thrust.

Head back, neck arched, I scream.

He pulls out and slams deep once again.

I'm broken.

I'm torn in two.

Yet, I want and need more of the burning flesh that I must strain to accept, more than I want my next breath. My hips strain to lift to meet his slow, determined thrusts. Each savage filling brings a flutter to my core. Teeth graze my throat as he growls over his prize.

He fucks me. Takes me roughly. Bound as I am, I find freedom that transcends my earthly body. The hard ground does not give; neither does the hard male flesh filling me over and over.

I am the softness caught between.

The fire rises again, the contractions low in my womb like a thousand tiny fists twisting the delicate flesh.

I taste blood.

My pussy convulses, severe contractions pulsing out slick around his thick flesh, and still he does not stop.

I sink my teeth deeper into hot male skin, and he growls his approval as I mark and claim him as my mate.

"Open for me," he says, but I do not know what he means, only that I need something more.

Aramis

The feeling of her tight cunt squeezing over my cock is the highest form of torment. My burgeoning knot, the highest form of pleasure. Her small teeth savage my chest, bringing a heated surge of male pride.

Cutting the ropes binding her ankles, I cant her ass, giving me a better angle.

"Goddess!"

Her cry accompanies my swelling knot. Each thrust into her gently clenching sheath sends the blood pulsing, engorging the flesh near the base until I can only force it in and out with gritted teeth. My balls feel heavy to the point of pain, but I want her sweet cunt stretched and gaping.

I want no doubt in her mind that she has been thoroughly claimed.

She begs me to come.

But I'm deep into my rut, and I think she can take more. She dared to try and run from me, and my darkness demands she be ravished in a way a willful omega deserves.

Nails rake over my flesh, and I welcome the sting.

Then she comes again, and the gentle clenching becomes a vise that draws the seed from my balls in thick, hot surges. I come. Over and over. My teeth seek her throat, sinking deep as I pin her thoroughly beneath me, holding her small body to mine, inside and out.

Body shuddering, feral grunts breathed against her bloody throat.

We are connected in a way that surpasses human intellect or words.

Linked irrevocably.

My cock pulses inside her, bathing the entrance to her womb, filling her until my seed leaks and drips all over her ruined gown.

As the knot softens, I free her bound wrists. The need to fuck her is already rising. As I stare down at her pretty, flushed face, I understand that I'm Goddess-blessed to have been given such a treasure. My lungs and chest are full in ways that have nothing to do with air. She is inside me even as I'm inside her.

I shudder as my cock slips out, and leaning back, inspect her ruined pussy. Her stomach ripples constantly, cum and slick trickling and pulsing as she continues to climax. Her body is limp, her chest rising and falling on a pant. One arm is flung over her eyes as if to hide from me. My lips twitch with amusement—my little doe has nowhere to hide.

I play in the spilled cum, scooping it up and forcing it back inside her with my fingers.

Goddess, she is so open—a captivating sight that brings an urgent thud to my cock.

I'm torn between watching her face she tries to hide contort with pleasure and her pink puffy cunt as I fuck my fingers in and out. When her hips start to rise in time with my thrusting fingers, my need to rut her again grows.

As I put her on her hands and knees, my last fleeting thought is to rut her so thoroughly that she will never dare to run from me again.

Chapter Four

Rosalind

Many hours have passed while I've been lost to my heat. Cognizance arrives like awakening from a surreal dream.

But it's not a dream. I'm naked, my body aches, even my skin feels tender to the touch. Warm flesh and prickly hair make a cushion for my cheek as I lay curled into Aramis's chest. The comforting weight of his arm anchors me to him while his thick, muscular thigh is wedged between mine. His scent and presence surround me. As I shift, I feel a different ache, deep inside my core where he has filled me over and over—I sigh.

He shifts with me, thigh pressing upward, the coarse hair abrasive as it rubs against my tender pussy and swollen clit. I hiss, but it turns into a groan as his hand tightens over my ass, and he grinds my softness against his hardness.

"My naughty little doe," he purrs against my temple. "Have you not been fucked enough?"

It's not him that is grinding, I realize, it's me. My hips

move of their own volition. Goddess, I'm so sore and used, yet there is pleasure too, and I'm greedy for more.

"Do you need to be filled again before we leave?"

Leave? I have questions, but they're of only fleeting importance for my body has needs. "Please." My pussy clenches and gushes over his thigh. This is not my heat anymore. This is all me.

"What a treasure I've found," he says. His hand slides down over my ass, through slick folds until it hovers at my entrance. Fingers rim my pussy, sending nerves rushing to life. "You're so open, love. Can you feel that? I think I might need to inspect you before I let you have my cock again."

I whimper. The magic fingers set need pounding; I'll suffer anything so long as Aramis eases this ache.

With my back to the ground, barely shielded by my filthy dress, I'm spread open for his view. A flush spreads over my cheeks, down my throat, and across the upper swell of my breasts.

His hooded gaze turns heated as he carefully parts my pussy lips. Thick fingers circle my entrance again. "Can you feel that, little doe? Feel how open you are?" A single finger presses inside, and I can feel how easily it enters. The wet squelching noises as he pumps slowly make me squirm. "Your pussy is gaping, love." He changes the movement, swiping his fingers from side to side to emphasize his filthy assessment. "Open and well-fucked, how an omega should be."

Goddess, the sounds and the sensation of being open are both horrifying and arousing.

"You'll need to take my cock here often, or you'll tighten up, and I'll need to start all over again."

"Please, I don't like it."

He plunges three fingers deeply, and my back arches

up. "Yes!"

"Is that better, love? Better when I fill you up?"

I whimper, my hips lifting in encouragement for him to ease the ache. "I need more. Please, Aramis. I need you inside me."

His fingers withdraw, and he rolls onto his back, lifting me over him. I growl my disapproval as exhausted thigh muscles are spread wide over his much larger bulk. My slick leaks over his firm abdominals, even this light stimulation as my clit slides over his firm flesh brings a groan to my lips. His cock, thick and heavy, pulses against my opening.

"My cock is yours," he says, grey eyes turning black. "Use it however you need."

I'm exhausted; my arms shake as I try to hold myself over him so that I might claim the hot flesh and fill this terrible emptiness. He doesn't help as he watches me struggle to lift myself onto his burning length.

My hands shake, my legs tremble. I'm near insensible with the strain of fitting the tip to my weeping entrance. A sob escapes me as his cock finally breeches me. "Goddess, yes!" I collapse, a scream tearing from my lips when his hard flesh spears savagely inside.

He purrs, rising up, his arms shackling my waist, keeping me locked upon his throbbing cock. "Hush, love, open for me."

Tears stream down my cheeks. The pulsing pain consumes me.

Gentle fingers brush knotty hair from my damp cheeks. The tenderness of his kiss against my temple goes to war with the fiery pain. He palms my throat, his other arm clamping tighter around my hips before he drags me up and slams me down.

"Oh!"

The pain explodes into pleasure. It consumes me one savage thrust at a time. I sob openly, sweet agony and joy at being filled, pussy fluttering and already close to the glorious peak. Our flesh slaps together. His great strength and my small size making it easy for him to fuck me on and off his cock.

"Do you need my knot, Princess? Do you need your hot little cunt to be forced open around my knot?"

"Please!"

I'm bounced off and on with greater vigor. I feel myself opening even more, feel the thick ridge sliding past my tight entrance with every wet slap.

"Grip me, Rosa. Clench like I taught you."

I try to do as he asks, feeling the swell growing, forcing him to slow until the bulbous knot locks.

White sparks dance behind my eyes, and pleasure blooms deep inside, spreading out over my skin in waves of pinpricks. My wild moans merge with his savage roar.

A hot flood fills me up.

He rocks me, rubbing my swollen clit against his crotch and bringing another pounding wave of heavenly contractions.

Mated and thoroughly ravished, I find happiness beyond earthly measure. It crashes over me like a great roaring wave, bringing tears of joy coursing down my cheeks.

Seeking lips meet and tongues entwine. Where our chests touch, I can feel two hearts beat in tandem.

When our lips part, our eyes meet, and I look at the man I've bonded to in wonder.

"I didn't know it would be like this," I say. His storm-grey eyes hold impossible beauty, and I know I'm Goddess-blessed to have found a love transcendent.

Aramis

Her words bring the feeling of fullness to my chest again. I started out looking for a duchy, now I see that Rosa is the highest form of treasure worth infinitely more. Easing from her warmth is a form of torture endured only with the knowledge that we shall soon be in a safer place where I may sate my need for her again.

But darkness is falling, and it is time for us to leave.

There are twigs and leaves in the hair of my little ravished doe. It takes all my considerable willpower not to fall upon her and ravish her all over again. I promise myself that the next time I fill her, it will be in the comfort of a home and nest.

But we are not yet home, and this Goddess-blessed interlude will not last. It's my duty to protect the gift I have been given.

Her pretty eyes watch me as I dress. My pants and boots are in a good state, but her dress has served as bedding for us and is utterly ruined.

I see her eyeing her ballgown as I gather my cloak from the horse's saddle. A pink flush covers her cheeks when I wrap her in my cloak and nothing else. Given I have taken her with such vigor over the passing night and day, I find her modesty endearing.

"Where are we going?" she asks.

She is so tiny as she stands before me, blue eyes gazing up at me with questions.

"Home," I say, my lips tugging up at her shocked expression.

Rosalind

"Home," he says with a familiar smirk upon his lips that I don't see as cruel anymore. Turning from me, he collects the saddle from the ground and settles it over his horse's back.

Where is home? Not here—not anywhere, for I have plunged us through the portal, and we can never go home again.

My brows draw together as I watch him tighten the girdle. "But we cannot go home," I say. I'm lost. A kind of lost that's as much about inside a person as outside.

The bridle comes next, slipping over the muzzle of his horse, bit sliding between teeth. Aramis is gentle as he slips it over ears and adjusts it against the mane. The horse snorts softly, nudging his master as he seeks attention.

Broad hands patting the neck of his gelding, Aramis turns to look at me. "You really did learn nothing of portal laws," he says dryly.

My chagrin rises. I'm about to demand that Aramis give me a straight answer, for I'm a princess and even an omega princess deserves a measure of respect. But my mouth opens and closes again without me uttering a word. His thorough claiming and the punishment are still fresh. My bottom aches a little where he spanked it, and I'm worried my poor pussy will never be the same again.

The mere thought of his ravishment brings a tightness to my womb that is both sharp and pleasurable in the darkest of ways.

Heat enters his pale eyes as the pupils grow until they almost swallow the storm-grey. "So, you can learn some lessons, Princess." He walks the horse over to me, and gathering my hand in his, guides us the short distance through the trees and back to the path.

I steel myself to see the slain beast, but I notice it is not there as we emerge.

I can only wonder for a moment because a faint shimmering grows in the middle of the path, growing, swirling, and condensing until it forms into a portal.

The portal.

"But how?" I turn to find Aramis studying me. It brings a tightness to my chest and a sense of wonder that this alpha is now my mate.

"I have heard that the Goddess can bestow gifts such as this on occasion," Aramis says. "I prayed that the portal might return."

I turn back to the shimmering portal. I'm fearful of passing through again, but I do not know this place, and I want desperately to return to the familiar lands I call home. "Will it really take us back?" I ask.

"There is only one way to find out," he says.

He lifts me up into the saddle, mounts behind me, and with a gentle click of his tongue, the horse moves forward.

My hand clutches his arm where it is wrapped protectively around me. As we draw closer, my pulse quickens and a clammy sickness roils in my gut.

"Close your eyes," he says softly.

I do.

I know the moment we make contact, the oily film that covers me and the absolute silence that swallows my scream. Then I feel Aramis, his arm still closed protectively around me, and I cling to the connection as we endure the in-between.

Chapter Five

Rosalind

Our exit from the portal is much gentler this time around. Still mounted, we emerge once more onto a mirror forest path.

I might imagine it to be a trick and yet another world but for the welcoming committee. My mother, father, a dozen castle guards, and Aramis's companion, Edgar, are waiting for us when we emerge. Horses are corralled to the right, and a rough camp of sorts has been set.

Tears fall swiftly. Wrapping the cloak tightly around my nakedness, Aramis lifts me down.

"My dear, sweet Rosalind," my mother says, drawing me into her arms and filling my lungs with the scent of lilies. "We've been worried beyond words. It was only Edgar's determination that Aramis was with you that gave us hope."

We both weep cathartic tears. I have been very foolish trying to escape my Goddess-blessed fate.

I hear my father talking to Aramis—my mate's companion, Edgar, joins them. The low tones of their conversation wash over me, although I cannot hear the words.

As my tears slow and I lift my head, I see a rueful smile on my mother's face. "My goodness," she says, tucking my hair behind my ear before showing me a leaf.

My blush consumes my whole body, and I tentatively try to smooth my knotty hair while retaining possession of my cloak.

"Do not mind it," she says with a wink. "Your scent has changed, thank the Goddess. Now your dear sister must find something new to complain about."

My laughter is filled with a warmth I've not felt in a long time. It was not only my mother who stopped smiling when my scent changed; it was also me.

My scent has changed.

Acknowledging this reminds me that I'm bound and mated now to the most formidable alpha I've ever met.

I sense his approach even before his heat and spicy pheromones reach me. A warm blanket is placed over the cloak, and although it is not cold, it comforts me. My mother steps away, returning to my father—they embrace, and I see all the love they feel for each other and for me in that touch.

Love.

It's the glue that holds families together. It's the most precious gift the Goddess can give.

Turning within his arms, my eyes search those of my alpha. "Where will we go?" I ask Aramis.

"We'll stay here with your parents until you're recovered fully from the ordeal," he says. "Then we will travel together to our new home in the shadows of the eastern mountains... My aunt has graced me with her blessing to inherit my late uncle's lands."

A cloud lowers over me. Shock perhaps.

No, it's more than that.

The man who wraps me so tenderly with the blanket before lifting me to his horse does not love me. I'm merely a means to an end for him.

※

Aramis

As I lift Rosalind onto my horse, I see the wariness enter her eyes.

Mounting behind her, I gather the reins and pull the blanket about her securely before we ride back to her childhood home and castle. She remains silent as we travel the short distance. I sense delayed shock, but also something more.

The mention of the duchy caused her sadness, and knowing this brings a heaviness to my chest.

I've thought of little beyond securing the duchy since I was informed of my uncle's will. And I've thought of little beyond the tiny omega who sits before me since the day we first met.

Now, and as I receive news that the lands are mine, I realize that my mate's happiness means more to me than any land.

A veritable crowd awaits us at the castle, and I keep her close to me and shield her as best I can from prying eyes. Taking her into my arms, I carry her, despite her protest, to her quarters here.

Setting her upon the bed, I allow the servants to bring food and drink before ordering them all out.

As the door clicks shut, bringing blessed aloneness, my eyes settle on my little doe.

The filthy little imp sits demurely upon the bed, lashes lowered as she wrings her hands. With a shake of my head at whatever quarrel is about to come, I strip out of my dirty clothes. A bath might be advisable for both of us, but I will address whatever is troubling her immediately, and with my cock buried in her hot little cunt if need be.

Wide eyes blink in the direction of my jutting cock as I stride toward the bed and my mate before she wrests her gaze away. I catch her before her flight takes her from the bed, rip the blanket and cloak from her, and, taking her chin in hand, force her to meet my eyes.

Sprawled out beneath me on the bed, with my body caging her, my little doe has nowhere to go.

"What is troubling you?" I ask.

Her face is flushed, and her eyes dip subconsciously to where my cock jerks enthusiastically like a spear targeting its favorite prey. I tap her chin to gain her attention lest this deteriorate and we fall upon one another again.

"Nothing," she says.

It's my firm belief that when a woman says nothing troubles them, something most assuredly does. My lips twitch, although it pains me to see her suffering so.

"Nothing?" I ask with an arched brow. Perhaps fucking her is the right answer. The *only* answer. I can scent her slick weeping... I wonder if her little pussy has already clamped shut. Why does the thought of it tightening bring forth depraved images of me ruining it all over again?

A small token struggle ensues as I line my cock with her little puffy entrance.

"Goddess," she whispers. "I'm still sore."

I thrust deep.

A growl erupts from my chest as I watch rapture contort her pretty face. "You have tightened up, my little doe," I say, clamping an arm around her waist so I can hold her still. Three good, deep drives into her softness, and I'm fully seated where I belong.

"Now," I say, brushing knotty hair from her hot cheeks. "Tell me what's wrong."

Rosalind

I don't want to talk to him, but I also don't have a choice. His cock is buried inside me, hot and pulsing. His huge body surrounds me, and his scent fills my lungs. I love him, and yet, how can I love him if he does not also love me?

Tears spill down my cheeks, and I strain, arching my back, twisting one way and then the other as I try to buck him off.

He lets me wear myself out. Pinning my wrists above my head, he grinds his cock into my softness, reminding me that I'm an omega and cannot possibly win this fight.

My rage leaves me as quickly as it arrives.

"You don't love me," I whisper, and this time I meet his eyes. "Everyone knows I'm a means to you gaining the duchy."

His eyes cloud and then darken, the transition so swift that I wonder if it's a trick of the light.

"Foolish woman," he says, taking my wrists within one hand, he uses the other to cup my cheek. "Do I act like a man interested only in a duchy?" His hips roll, sliding his cock out before slamming it back in. "Does this feel like I have no interest in you, mate?"

His eyes lock with mine, and I cannot look away. He begins to fuck me, slow, steady slaps as our bodies come together. Inside, I'm so sore, and yet, it's the most bittersweet pleasure I have known. Each fierce joining of our flesh drives a greater understanding that I love him with all my heart.

"A man does not wade into the portal for a chance to win a duchy. I could have wed a dozen other willing betas a month ago were that my only desire." The thrusts increase. Our gusty breaths mingle. I'm trapped as much by the look in his eyes as by his body and the thick length that fills me over and over again. "I've had my horse ten years; I fucking love that ugly beast, but I'd have flogged him to exhaustion were it necessary to reach you in time."

My lips tremble and tears swim before my eyes.

"I love you, you foolish, willful, Goddess-blessed little doe. I would plunge after you into hell to keep you safe and spend eternity battling the minions there." Stilling deep inside me, he presses my palm to his chest. "Feel here. Feel how my heart beats for you."

"I feel it," I say—tears stream down my face. We're connected in every way. My chest fills with my love for him, and under my fingers, his does the same.

He shifts, bringing awareness back to our joined bodies, and a groan escapes from my lips. "I love you," I say, only it manifests a fierce urge to mark what is mine. My teeth seek the place on his chest where I have already made my claim, only this time, I want to go deeper.

He growls softly as I sink my teeth in, and deep inside, I feel the knot blooming the harder I bite. I taste blood, but he only cups the back of my head and encourages me to take more.

"Mark your mate, love," he growls. "I am yours until the Goddess claims us both."

His hips rock against me, bringing a sweet, dark pleasure rising as his knot swells, filling my entrance and triggering my release. I bask in the heavenly contractions, feeling him pulse as hot seed fills me.

We stay like that for many minutes, lost in the connection.

"What will happen now?" I ask.

"What do you want to happen?" he counters, taking my dirty hand and inspecting it with mock disgust. "I think a bath might be in order, and then I will spend as many hours as is necessary fucking you until you are good and bred," he says with a sinful smirk.

I giggle. "I think I could suffer through such a fate." My face turns serious, for I have damaged this growing love by doubting him. "What about your duchy? Will we live there?"

"Only if you wish," he says, eyes narrowing. "Although, it will pain me to see it go to my hapless cousin, who knows nothing about defending such a vulnerable estate. Your happiness is more important. Did I not already make that clear? Do I need to fuck you to the point of exhaustion before you believe me?" His lips find the claiming mark at my throat, sucking against it sharply, teeth grazing with threatening intent.

I know little of his cousin, but I'd heard that the duchy suffered raiding to autumn supply routes. I don't like the thought of living somewhere so dangerous, but I also believe he was gifted the duchy for a reason.

The people there deserve the best lord, one who will keep them safe in times of trouble.

"I would like to go to the duchy," I say.

I yelp as he nips at the claiming mark.

He lifts his head, and my breath catches as I see all the hunger and love in his eyes.

"Then we shall go there," he says.

Then his lips tug up and his eyes promise the wickedness I have already come to crave. "But first I need to remind my mate how much I love and need her."

Dragging my small body under his, and to my great pleasure, he does precisely that.

Did you enjoy Ravished? Please consider leaving a review. Authors love reviews!

What is next from Coveted Prey?
How about some spicy barbarians... Trained For Their Pleasure!

For free short stories, please check out BOOKS | FREE READS on my website www.AuthorLVLane.com

Enjoying my writing? You can find my latest WIP in serial format by becoming a Patron https://reamstories.com/lvlane

Also by L.V. Lane

Coveted Prey

Prey

Prize

Taken

Trained For Their Pleasure

Claimed For Their Pleasure

Rapture

Centaur in My Forest

Claimed by Three

Bound to the Pack

Centaur in my Valley

The Centaur in My Dreams

Captured by the Wolven

Tempting the Orc

Stolen by Darkness

Traded for Their Pleasure

Melody Unbound

Bound for their Pleasure

Gentling the Beast

The Coveted Beta

Beauty and the Bears

The Controllers

The Awakening
Taking Control
Complete Control
Deviant Control
Deviant Evolution
Deviant Betrayl
Ruthless Control
Absolute Control
Deviant Games
Savage Control

Mate for the Alien Master

Punished
Ravaged
Avenged
Gifted to the Gladiator

The Girl with the Gray Eyes

The Girl with the Gray Eyes
The Warrior in the Shadows
The Master of the Switch

Darkly Ever After

Owned

Owned and Knotted

Verity Arden

Enjoyed L.V.'s books? You might also enjoy her contemporary pen name, Verity Arden!

In His Debt

Make Her Purr

Good With His Hands

Rough Around The Edges

About the Author

In a secret garden hidden behind a wall of shrubs and trees, you'll find L.V. Lane's writing den, where she crafts adventures in fantastical worlds.

Best known for spicy adventures...Magical and mythical creatures, wolf shifters, and alphas of every flavor who give sweet and feisty omegas and heroines a guaranteed HEA, she also writes the occasional character-driven hard sci-fi full of political intrigue and action.

Subscribe to my mailing list at my website for the latest news: www.AuthorLVLane.com

- facebook.com/LVLaneAuthor
- x.com/AuthorLVLane
- instagram.com/authorlvlane
- amazon.com/author/lvlane
- bookbub.com/profile/l-v-lane
- goodreads.com/LVLane

Printed in Great Britain
by Amazon